I'm still here in the bathtub

To those who keep my bathtub overflowing with love—my wonderful wife,
Rose, and our amazing kids: Simone, Andrew, Nathan, and David
—A. K.

To Mom and Dad
—D. C.

Margaret K. McElderry Books
An imprint of Simon & Schuster Children's Publishing Division
1230 Avenue of the Americas
New York, NY 10020

Text copyright © 2003 by Alan Katz
Illustrations copyright © 2003 by David Catrow

Book design by Sonia Chaghatzbanian
The text of this book is set in Kosmik.
The illustrations are rendered in watercolors, colored pencil, and ink.

Manufactured in China

10 9 8 7 6 5 4 3 2 1

Library of Congress Cataloging-in-Publication Data
Katz, Alan.
I'm still here in the bathtub : brand new silly dilly songs / by Alan Katz ;
illustrated by David Catrow.
p. cm.
Summary: Well-known songs, including "Itsy Bitsy Spider" and "Farmer in the Dell," are presented
with new words and titles, such as "Tiny Baby Brother" and "I'm in My Room and Bored."
ISBN: 0-689-84551-0
1. Children's songs—United States—Texts. 2. Humorous songs—Texts. [1. Humorous songs.
2. Songs.]
I. Catrow, David, ill. II. Title.
PZ8.3.K1275 Im 2003
782.42164'0268—dc21
[E]
2001051208

I'm still here in the bathtub

brand new silly dilly songs

by Alan Katz

illustrated by David Catrow

Margaret K. McElderry Books

New York London Toronto Sydney Singapore

I'm Still Here in the Bathtub

(To the tune of "Take Me Out to the Ballgame")

I'm still here in the bathtub
I'm so clean that I squeak
Mom says it's good to relax and soak
It's been two days . . . there's no room to breaststroke
Oh, this bathtub is like an island
On which I have been marooned
I am wrink-, wrink-, wrinkled so much
You can call me Prune!

I'm still here in the bathtub
My washcloth is just threads
Soap is all gone and there's no shampoo
Please lend a hand or just send a canoe
I know cleanliness is important
And I don't mean to complain
If I can't get outta this tub
I'll go down the drain!

I'm still here in the bathtub
Now it feels like a week
How many times do I have to rinse?
I scrubbed away all my fi-in-ger-prints
Oh, I think somebody is coming
There's now a knock at the door
Hello, Mom, no, don't take me out
Just five minutes more!

I-T-C-H-Y

(To the tune of "Bingo")

I got a sweater made of wool
It's hot and boy, it's itchy
I–T–C–H–Y
Gee, I want to cry
Why'd my parents buy
An itchy, twitchy sweater?

I got some shoes with shiny soles
They're chic, but oh, they're squeaky
S–Q–U–EAK–EAK
Folks can't hear me speak
I would like to sneak
'Em on our Irish setter!

I got a hat with stupid flaps
That cover up my eardrums
No way can I hear
No one's voice is clear
It's so bad, I fear
Should write my mom a letter!

My gloves are thick, my hood is tight
My pants fall down, can't take it
Don't call me a pest
But the way I'm dressed
Think it would be best
Just to go outside naked!

Aunt Bea Says

(To the tune of "The Alphabet Song")

Aunt Bea says, "Oh, golly gee!"
Then she starts to bear-hug me
"Ouch!" I yell
I can't flee
There's no way
To break free
She can't hear my yells and pleas
'Cause she's got me in a squeeze!

Cousin Jim says, "Let him be!"
But Aunt Bea does not agree
Her hug's like
An attack
I can feel
My ribs crack
And my eyes pop out like peas
She owes me apologies!

It gets worse when Aunt Marie
Reaches in and rescues me
Slobbers like
A wet pooch
When she gives
Me a smooch
Cuckoo birds, it seems to me,
Fly around our family tree!

Tiny Baby Brother

(To the tune of "Itsy Bitsy Spider")

My tiny baby brother
Took our remote control
When I wasn't looking
He flushed it down the bowl
Mom said it's my fault
And when I watch him again
Then my tiny baby brother
Must stay in his playpen!

Again today I baby-sat
And figured, it's okay
Reached in, plucked him out
Let him run away
He smashed our mother's car phone
Smeared paint throughout the den
That's why I'm singing this song
From inside his playpen!

I'm a Menace

(To the tune of "Frère Jacques")

I'm a menace
I played tennis
In my house
In my room
Didn't know a racket
Could hit a lamp and crack it
I smell doom
In my room!

Life is rocky
I played hockey
Against Clyde
While inside
Scored—and broke a window
Now I feel the wind blow
While inside
Gotta hide!

I was naughty
Did karate
I showed Ben
In the den
Thanks to all my chopping
We're VCR-shopping
For the den
Once again.

I'm athletic
It's pathetic
Mom gets sore
More and more
Though it's aggravating
Let's both go ice-skating
Kitchen floor
Fun galore!

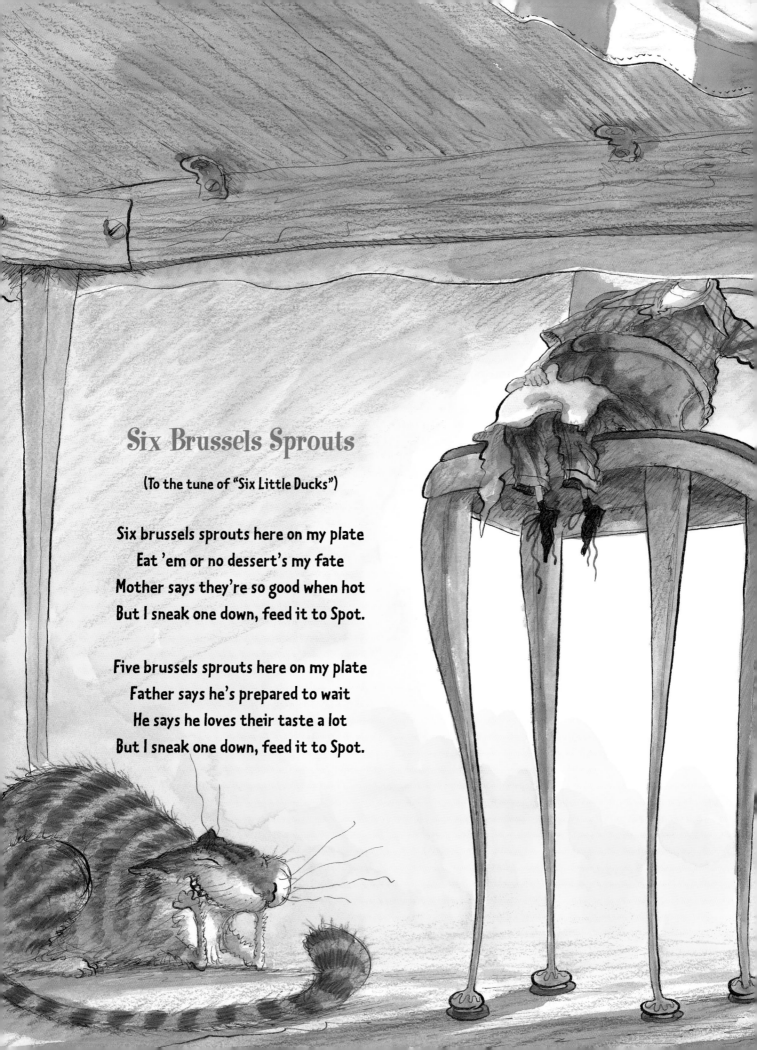

Six Brussels Sprouts

(To the tune of "Six Little Ducks")

Six brussels sprouts here on my plate
Eat 'em or no dessert's my fate
Mother says they're so good when hot
But I sneak one down, feed it to Spot.

Five brussels sprouts here on my plate
Father says he's prepared to wait
He says he loves their taste a lot
But I sneak one down, feed it to Spot.

Four brussels sprouts here on my plate
Want to avoid this big stalemate
Mom goes to get the gravy pot
And I sneak one down, feed it to Spot.

Three brussels sprouts here on my plate
Halfway through this food debate
Eating them is a real long shot
So I sneak one down, feed it to Spot.

Two brussels sprouts here on my plate
Two slimy balls to eliminate
I'm proving I'm not a fusspot
So I sneak one down, feed it to Spot.

One brussels sprout here on my plate
What a great dog to cooperate
I just bent down and did you-know-what
Fed the last brussels sprout to Spot!

No brussels sprouts here on my plate
Mother says time to celebrate
Then the sad truth is I got caught
All six sprouts were coughed up by Spot.

I Always Lose

(To the tune of "Skip to My Lou")

Lost my parka, what'll I do?
Plus my backpack, and my left shoe
To my tuba, it's toodle-oo
My folks'll sure be snarling!

Turned around, lunch box was gone
Could've sworn I had a hat on
There's no sign of baby bro Ron
He's a pain, but he's darling.

Lose, lose, my stuff I lose
Lose, lose, I got no clues
Lose, lose, lost my tattoos
Mom says that it's appalling!

Parka, shoe, backpack, and hat
Lunch box, tuba, where's Ron at?
They're all gone . . . oops, so's the cat
Gotta go, Dad is calling!

Lose, lose, he blew a fuse
Lose, lose, it's all bad news
Lose, lose, wish I could choose
To lose the losing . . . I'm bawling!

No Medication

(To the tune of "Down by the Station")

No medication
Don't care what the doc says
Won't put that stuff in my belly
Tastes bad, you know
Mom sticks it in ice cream
Thinks that she can fool me
I flick it out the window
Look out below!

No medication
Though my throat is aching
Good for me, but yuck, it's smelly
So I must say no
Dad hands me a milk shake,
But he mixed it in there
Back to the window
Watch it go!

I'm not a good patient
Guess I never listen
Hey, here comes our neighbor
This will not be fun
On her head is ice cream
Her shirt is full of milk shake
I'll taste my own medicine
In more ways than one!

He's Got the Whole Beach in His Pants

(To the tune of "He's Got the Whole World in His Hands")

My brother played down in the sand
He had a lot of cool shovels in his hand
But now home he's jumpin' like a rubber band
He's got the whole beach in his pants!

He's got the whole beach in his pants
When he takes 'em off, a clam'll do a dance
If you change his diaper, there is quite a chance
You'll find a lobster in his pants!

Though some people take shells as souvenirs
He's got a ton of sand in his hair and ears
He's the reason that they say the coast is clear
Think he should sleep at the pier!

The Meals at My Camp

(To the tune of "Wheels on the Bus")

The meals at my camp
I can't explain
I got pain
In my brain
Can't tell if it's fish,
Meat, or chow mein
Each day at camp!

The breakfast at my camp
Is cooked by Greg
We all beg
Please, no egg!
So runny it just runs down my leg
All through the camp!

The lunches at my camp
Prepared by Joan
Didn't know
Cheese had bones
Her specialty is tuna ice-cream cones
Each day at camp!

The dinners at my camp
Are made by Trish
Toss the food
Eat the dish
For my parents I have got one wish
Next year, new camp!

My Friend Donald

(To the tune of "Old MacDonald")

My friend Donald meant no harm
He's a pal, you know
We were just playing hospital
I said, "I hurt my toe."
He said, "Operate!"
But I yelled, "Hey, wait!
Hold it, Doc! It's a rock!
Stuck inside my left sock!"
My friend Donald meant no harm
Still, I told him whoa!

My friend Donald's catfish parm
Tasted like Play–Doh
When we were playing restaurant
It made my stomach glow!
I yelled "Ouch ouch!" here
I cried "Ouch ouch!" there
Boy, it hurt
"Here's some dirt,"
He said, "It's your dee–ssert!"
My friend Donald's catfish parm
Don't eat it, no no!

Bad Advice

(To the tune of "Three Blind Mice")

Bad advice
Bad advice
That's what I gave
To my friend Dave
I told him he should shampoo with dirt
To gym class just wear a hula skirt
I said eat broccoli for dessert
That's bad advice
At any price!

Bad advice
Bad advice
Such fun to give
To my friend Viv
Till teacher found out that I'm the fool
Who said to throw a fish in the pool
If you don't want to stay after school
Take my advice
Don't take my advice!

My Sister Fights With Me

(To the tune of "My Country 'Tis of Thee")

My sister fights with me
We always disagree
And it's her fault!
She breaks my favorite stuff
She treats me mean and rough
I say, "I've had enough!"
Our mom yells halt!

So we act like we're friends
But soon the niceness ends
She starts to hiss
Taking things from my drawers
Making me do her chores
And worst of all, she snores
Please take my sis!

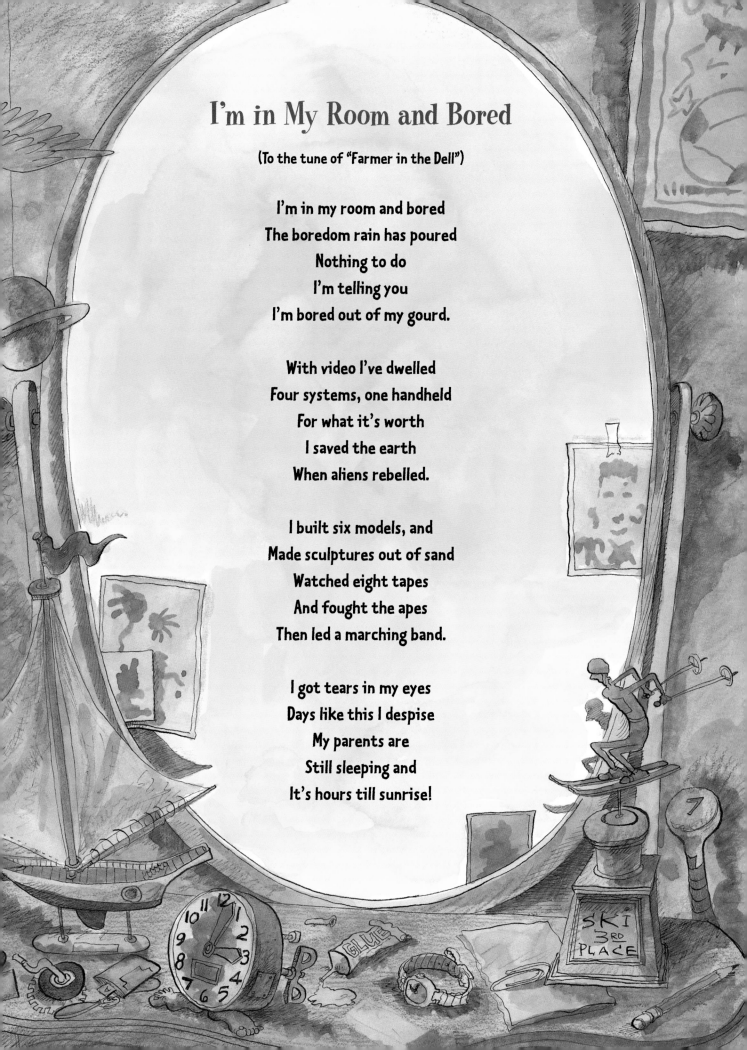

I'm in My Room and Bored

(To the tune of "Farmer in the Dell")

I'm in my room and bored
The boredom rain has poured
Nothing to do
I'm telling you
I'm bored out of my gourd.

With video I've dwelled
Four systems, one handheld
For what it's worth
I saved the earth
When aliens rebelled.

I built six models, and
Made sculptures out of sand
Watched eight tapes
And fought the apes
Then led a marching band.

I got tears in my eyes
Days like this I despise
My parents are
Still sleeping and
It's hours till sunrise!